AGENT Amelia Spooky Ballet!

AGENT Amelia

Spooky Ballet!

Agent Amelia
#4

MICHAEL BROAD

MINNEAPOLIS

American edition published in 2011 by Darby Creek, a division of Lerner Publishing Group, Inc.

Copyright © 2009 by Michael Broad

First published in 2009 by Andersen Press Limited,
20 Vauxhall Bridge Road, London SW1V 2SA
www.andersenpress.co.uk
www.michaelbroad.co.uk

Darby Creek
A division of Lerner Publishing Group, Inc.
241 First Avenue North
Minneapolis, MN 55401 U.S.A.

Website address: www.lernerbooks.com

Library of Congress Cataloging-in-Publication Data

Broad, Michael.
    Spooky ballet! / written and illustrated by Michael Broad. — American ed.
        v.   cm. — (Agent Amelia, #4)
    Summary: Young Amelia, a secret agent, investigates a class of entranced ballet students, a scarecrow that can control crows, and a librarian whose work on the school library's computers seems to turn students into robots.
    Contents: The case of the spooky ballet — The case of the whistling scarecrow — The case of the gobbledygook books.
    ISBN: 978–0–7613–8059–7 (lib. bdg. : alk. paper) [1. Spies—Fiction. 2. Ballet dancing—Fiction. 3. Scarecrows—Fiction. 4. Computer crimes—Fiction.] I. Title.
PZ7.B780834Fo 2011
[E]—dc22   2011001088

Manufactured in the United States of America
1 – BP – 7/15/11

For Tina

I'M AMELIA KIDD and I'm a secret agent.

Well, I'm not actually a secret agent. I don't work for the government or anything. But I've saved the world loads of times from evil geniuses and criminal masterminds. There are loads of them around if you know what to look for.

I'm really good at disguises. I make my own gadgets (which sometimes work), and I'm used to improvising in sticky situations—which you have to do all the time when you're a secret agent.

These are my Secret Agent Case Files.

The Case of the Spooky Ballet

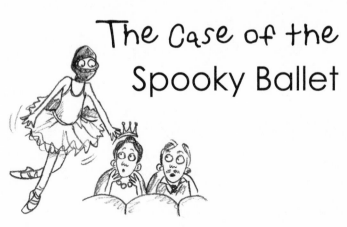

When you're a secret agent, it's always a good idea to have some martial-art skills. Evil geniuses and criminal masterminds can turn pretty nasty when you foil their plans to take over the world.

The local community recreation center advertised loads of different classes in karate and jujitsu. After a week of dropping hints, Mom finally signed me up for an evening class!

Although, she was very vague about exactly *which* martial art I would be studying ...

When we drove up to the rec center, there were already a few girls waiting around outside. I thought it was really cool that so many girls had signed up for martial arts. I did expect to see *some* boys though.

"I'll pick you up here in two hours," Mom said cheerily, as I got out of the car.

"But you still haven't told me which . . ." I didn't get to finish what I was saying because  Mom waved enthusiastically and sped away. I couldn't help noticing that she was grinning from ear to ear.

"Hmmm," I thought. I pulled on my backpack and headed for the entrance.

The group of girls were gathered around outside the doors. I froze on the spot when I heard a familiar voice coming from the middle of the huddle.

It was loud and shrill and seemed to
be demanding something.

"Of course she'll pick me!" it
shrieked. "You all are like clumsy
hippopotamuses!"

As the girls backed away, I saw
Trudy Hart at the center! Trudy is my
arch nemesis at school. She's not an
evil genius or a criminal mastermind,

but she is very spoiled and used to getting her way!

When Trudy saw me coming toward them, she abandoned whatever she was yelling about and barged past the other girls. She strode up to me and poked me with her finger.

"What are *you* doing here?" Trudy demanded.

"I'm here for the class, of course," I said calmly.

"You're training with Madam Giselle?" Trudy chuckled. "Well, this I *have* to see!"

I was about to ask who Madam Giselle was when the doors to the rec center burst open. Standing in the doorway was a crooked old woman with a long black cane.

"Enter!" she roared dramatically and then scuttled back inside.

Trudy hurried forward to get inside before anyone else. I tagged along behind. Madam Giselle was obviously the class teacher, but I really couldn't see her delivering a decent karate kick!

Inside the hall everyone started getting changed. As the girls put up their hair, pulled on their tutus, and tied the ribbons on their satin shoes, everything suddenly became clear.

My mom is *always* trying to make me do girly things like flower arranging or embroidery.

She doesn't know I'm a secret agent off saving the world all the time. Now she'd actually *tricked me* into taking ballet lessons!

Seeing the girls fluffing out their identical pink tutus, it occurred to me that there was still a way out. I couldn't be a ballerina in combat pants and running shoes. I quickly approached Madam Giselle.

"Er, I don't have a tutu or ballet shoes," I sighed, pretending to look disappointed.

"You must be Amelia Kidd," sniffed Madam Giselle. She eyed me up and down.

I nodded and tried to ignore Trudy making faces behind the old woman's back.

"I told your mother that all my dancers wear my own *specially designed* tutus and ballet shoes!" said

Madam Giselle. She jabbed her cane at a mass of pink frills hanging on the wall behind her. "And *those* are yours!"

"Great!" I sighed, taking down the dress.

The other girls were chatting while I got changed. I soon discovered that as well as being in the wrong class, I was also several weeks behind. The girls were already dancing *Swan Lake*. Madam Giselle was about to select the prima ballerina—the star dancer.

"And I'm also the most beautiful!" declared Trudy Hart. She had just listed all the reasons why she and no one else was qualified for prima ballerina status. "So there will be big trouble if Madam Giselle doesn't pick me!"

With everyone changed,
Madam Giselle scuttled to the center
of the studio. She tapped her black
cane twice on the wooden floor.

TAP! TAP!

All the girls fluttered forward and
stood in a line on tippy toes.

I stumbled forward feeling miserable and weighed down by frills.

Tugging at the tutu, I couldn't help wondering why it was so heavy for something so frilly. I wondered if the "special design" included weights in the waistband, as it was also pretty lumpy. I was about to complain when Madam Giselle spoke.

"The prima ballerina is the star of the show!" she said, with a faraway look in her eyes. "I was once the prima ballerina at the King's Theater, until I was cut down in my prime! When I turned a mere *seventy* years old, they said I was too old. . . ."

"Oh, get on with it!" growled Trudy.

Madam Giselle narrowed her eyes at Trudy. Then she waved the rest of her story away with an elegant swoosh of the hand.

She smiled unconvincingly and then produced a large white tutu. It was twice as wide and frilly as the pink ones we were wearing and had two lengths of ribbon hanging down the sides.

Madam Giselle hobbled along the line of dancers. Each girl sighed heavily as the tutu passed by. When it eventually stopped at Trudy, it took all her effort not to snatch it from the old woman's hands.

"Trudy Hart," said Madam Giselle. "You will be our star!"

In a blur of movement, Trudy ripped off the pink tutu, tossed it over her shoulder, and wrapped the crisp white lace around her waist. She seemed to sag slightly as though this tutu was even heavier than the pink ones. But she managed to keep her head high enough to look down on the rest of us.

"Now we have much work to do!" snapped Madam Giselle, returning to the center of the studio. "So you must listen very carefully— exactly as we rehearsed!" she added, lifting the cane and tapping it on the floor again.

TAP! TAP
  TAP! TAP!
TAP!
  TAP! TAP!

Being a secret agent, I've studied Morse code—which is an old-fashioned alphabet of dots and dashes for tapping out messages. This tap, tap, tapping sounded very similar.

With every sequence of taps, the girls moved in perfect time with one another. They spun on their tippy toes, springing up and down with weird arm movements.

Madam Giselle nodded with satisfaction at each girl in turn. Then she frowned when she got to me.

"Listen to the cane!" she demanded, indicating that I should step in time with the TAP! TAP! TAP! "Surrender to the tap, tap, tapping!" she whispered.

It was at this point that I suspected something strange was going on. Usually I'm pretty quick to spot an evil genius or a criminal mastermind, but I'd been so horrified to find myself enrolled in ballet class that I'd ignored all the signs!

The "specially designed" tutus!
The bitter ballet story!
The Morse code cane!

I made a point of not surrendering to the tapping cane. I watched the hand movements of the other dancers instead. It was then that I realized these were not graceful ballet moves at all! The dancers looked like the grabbing claws of a junkyard crane!

With Madam Giselle standing next to me, I got a good look at the cane. For the first time, I noticed a small red button in the silver knob at the top.

Uh Oh!

Red buttons are very popular with those attempting to take over the world. I've come up against a few in my time, and every one made *something* explode. I wasn't sure what would explode if this button was pressed. I decided to play along while I figured it out.

The looks on the faces of the other girls seemed more vacant than usual. It seemed that the tapping cane had taken over their brains.

I slowly adjusted my expression to look as clueless as the rest of them. I tried my best to copy their moves.

It was really hard work spinning and bobbing and grabbing at the same time. Finally, I managed to convince Madam Giselle that I was a brainwashed ballerina. She stepped away from me looking very pleased with herself. Then she adjusted the rhythm of taps.

TAP! TAP! TAP! TAP! TAP! TAP! TAP! TAP! TAP! TAP! TAP!

TAP! TAP! TAP! TAP! TAP!

There seemed to be twice as many instructions as the cane jabbed the floor like a sewing-machine needle! Suddenly Trudy leaped away with a series of impressive jumps and spins. The next girl followed and then the next, until it was my turn to do the same.

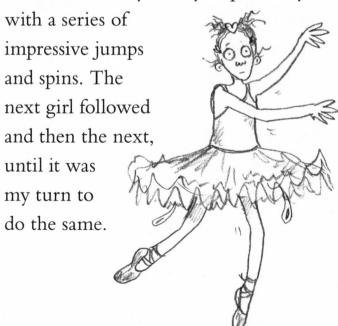

Fortunately, Madam Giselle was no longer focusing just on me. She didn't notice that my jumps and spins were not quite so graceful.

The ballerina train snaked around the studio. Each dancer made her weird movements while the teacher watched intently. She spent most of her time watching Trudy. The prima ballerina had no idea that she was starring in something dodgy and possibly explosive.

Once she was satisfied that all the dancers would respond to every instruction, Madam Giselle slowed the tap tempo. Everyone moved back into a line. Then she paused and made three rapid taps that obviously meant stop.

I was glad for the chance to rest. The dancing was really hard work. I ached all over. A quick glance sideways confirmed that the other girls were still in a trance, which meant I couldn't collapse into an exhausted heap!

"I think it is time for you all to wear your special ballet hats!" said Madam Giselle, mostly to herself as the spooky ballerinas stared straight ahead. She produced a cloth sack and handed something dark and fuzzy to each of the dancers. We all pulled on the headgear. The special "ballet hat" was actually a ski mask!

Beneath the mask, my vacant
expression turned to one of shock. I
realized that hiding our faces meant
we were leaving the hall. Whatever
Madam Giselle was planning was
happening now!

The old teacher scuttled up and
down, checking shoe ribbons and
straightening tutus. Then she pulled
on her own ski mask and leaped on
Trudy's back! The ribbons on Trudy's
dress turned out to be stirrups.

The old woman slipped her pointy,
black shoes through them.

Perched on Trudy's back, Madam Giselle tugged on her cane, and it extended to twice its length. She began tapping out new instructions that sent Trudy leaping through the doors of the hall. She was soon followed by the rest of the dancers.

It was hard work keeping up. The line of ballerinas bounded down Main Street like frilly gazelles, while avoiding startled shoppers who had to dive out of our way. A few onlookers actually applauded as we passed. They thought this was some strange kind of street performance.

With a few well-timed spins, I managed to twirl myself to the front of the regular dancers. There I could keep an eye on Trudy and her ridiculous rider, who was holding on with one hand and tapping the cane with the other.

Madam Giselle looked like a crazed crow perched on a wedding cake!

I still had no idea what the demented dancer was planning—or where we were going. Then I spied a poster stuck to a lamppost advertising *Swan Lake*!

This was a bit too much of a coincidence. With a sideways leap, I snatched it.

TONIGHT!
KING'S
THEATER
SWAN LAKE

Apparently a new production of *Swan Lake* was opening that night at the King's Theater. Madam Giselle was herding us straight for the people she blamed for ruining her ballet career!

Suddenly, the old woman steered Trudy down an alley at the side of the theater. Madam Giselle opened the stage door with a rusty old key. She ushered us inside, where the *Swan Lake* music was already playing. She made her frilly white filly gallop toward the stage!

Uh Oh!

I managed to stay close behind and focused on the cane. I had to nab it before the old woman pressed the red button. I got really close as they neared the wooden platform, but when I grabbed for it, Trudy did a massive leap like a zombie kangaroo. The next thing I knew we were all onstage!

The audience gasped when the ski-mask ballerinas appeared out of nowhere. The *real* ballerina misjudged a jump and landed on her bottom! Madam Giselle quickly dismounted Trudy and hobbled to the front of the stage!

"I have danced my whole life for you ungrateful people!" she roared. She snapped her cane back to its regular size and waved it at the stunned audience. "And now you will all pay!"

I charged to the front of the stage as the old woman lifted the cane to eye level. Her crooked thumb hovered over the silver knob.

But just as I went to snatch it, she pressed the red button!

Luckily, nothing exploded. Instead, the theater was filled with a whirring sound. When I looked down, I saw my tutu beginning to rotate! I quickly grabbed at the spinning frills. After a bit of wrestling, it ground to a halt and the motor in the waistband went

"POP!"

Looking around I noticed all
the other tutus were now at full
speed. Madam Giselle tapped out new
instructions that sent the ballerinas
into the audience. The spinning skirts
allowed the girls to leap from seat to
seat and hover above the
crowd as they picked
their pockets and stole
their jewelry.

"Money!"
I gasped. "You
want them to
'pay' with
money?"

For the
first time,
Madam Giselle
noticed that
one of her
ballerinas

was not doing as she was told. She
tapped even more frantically with the
cane, but I just folded my arms and
frowned.

"So you're just a regular
old thief?" I said. I was a bit
disappointed that she'd gone to such
insane effort just to rob people.

"You're not trying to take over the world with an army of brainwashed ballerinas?"

"Take over the world?" said the old woman, scratching her woolly chin. "No, of course not. But now you come to mention it, I could easily modify the cane controls and gather more girls. . . ."

"Oh, give me that!" I snapped.
I snatched the cane and tapped it three
times.

The ballerinas immediately
stopped plundering the audience and
dropped all the loot. But they were
still hovering in the air. They looked
pretty spooky, like frilly pink ghosts
in black ski masks!

I pressed the red button. The motors turned off and lowered the dancers to the floor. And it was just in time too because that was when I heard the police sirens wailing down Main Street.

When you're a secret agent, you can't take credit for saving the world—or even for saving a theater full of people from being robbed by a madwoman. You also have to protect the innocent, so I tapped the cane to bring the ballerinas back to the stage.

The tapping instructions were *very* similar to Morse code. I extended the cane and hopped onto Trudy's back for the getaway—*only* because I couldn't tap and run at the same time, of course.

Madam Giselle shook her fists
at me as we bounded away, but she
couldn't escape without the cane.
She had to stay in the spotlight
until the police arrested her.

I'd have to say she looked more like *Sitting Duck* than *Swan Lake*!

Back at the studio, I removed all the ski masks and broke the cane in half. The weary dancers snapped out of their trance. Luckily, they remembered nothing and were all too exhausted to care when I told

them Madam Giselle wouldn't be continuing the class. Well, all but one . . .

"But I'm the prima ballerina!" Trudy squealed. "The star of the show!"

"Sorry, I had to steal the show!" I laughed and headed for the door.

Mom was pretty sheepish when
I returned to the car. I didn't give her
a hard time about tricking me though.
Because not only had I *sort of* saved
the world again, but I'd also learned
some brilliant leaps and twirls that
would definitely come in handy on
secret-agent missions.

The Case of the Whistling Scarecrow

On sunny days, Mom sometimes
packs a picnic and drives us out to
the country. We find a nice, quiet
meadow away from the road. We lay
a blanket under a tree, and then we
relax all day long. Mom enjoys getting
away from the hustle and bustle. I
enjoy getting away from evil geniuses
and criminal masterminds trying to
take over the world.

Having spotted a peaceful meadow, we unpacked the car. We made our way down a winding path with the picnic basket and blanket. I also had my trusty backpack. A secret agent has to be prepared for anything.

Which was just as well . . .

As we climbed over a fence into the meadow, there was another family coming toward us with a picnic basket and blankets. Instead of looking happy and relaxed, they looked terrified.

"LEAVE THIS PLACE!" the mother warned, flapping her arms dramatically.

"Excuse me?" Mom gasped, as they bustled past.

"The phantom picnic thief has struck!" she said. She quickly clambered over the fence, followed by the rest of her family. "We packed a delicious picnic with sandwiches and cake and apple pie. Now we have nothing!"

I was about to quiz them on the specifics of the buffet burglary, but they were gone before I had a chance. They ran down the road as fast as their legs would carry them.

It was then that I saw a notice nailed to the fence post.

BEWARE
OF THE PHANTOM
PICNIC THIEF!
Any food brought
into this meadow
is likely to
mysteriously
vanish!

I snatched the piece of paper before Mom saw it. I stuffed it in my pocket.

Even though I was supposed to be having a day off, it was my duty as a secret agent to investigate the mystery.

 But first I had to convince Mom that this was still the perfect spot for a picnic.

"How rude!" I said. "That family *obviously* wants the whole place to themselves!"

"What do you mean?" Mom gasped. She looked completely bewildered.

"They must have seen us coming down the lane with our picnic basket!" I said. I pretended to sound shocked and appalled. "So they made up that silly story about a phantom to scare us off!"

"But they've left," Mom frowned. The fleeing family had disappeared around the corner.

"That's just what they *want* us to think," I said, tipping my sunglasses. "They're probably hiding behind a bush until we leave. Then they'll come back again. Well, we'll show them!" I headed straight for the tree in the middle of the meadow.

I'm not sure Mom was *entirely* convinced by my story—but the alternative was to admit that she believed in the phantom picnic thief! So she reluctantly followed me into the field.

Once we'd laid out the blanket and had a glass of lemonade, Mom seemed to forget all about the other family and their bizarre warning. The spot we'd chosen was bright and pretty. It looked like the most innocent place in the world.

When Mom
took out her book
and began reading,
it was time for me
to go to work. I
scanned the hilly
meadow for any
likely hiding places
like trees and hedges, where a food
thief might hide. But the area was
completely open. Then I turned my
attention to the neighboring farm
fields. I narrowed my eyes at
the scarecrows scattered
along the edge.

"I think I'll go and pick some wildflowers," I said whimsically. I grabbed an extra pointy pencil from my backpack. I took some paper too so it would look like I planned to do some drawing, but I had other plans for the pencil. . . .

"OK, darling," Mom said, peering over her book. "But stay where I can see you."

"I will," I said. I casually made my way toward the nearest field.

Skipping along the fence at the edge of the field, I paused at each scarecrow and gave it a quick jab in the leg with the pencil. I wanted to make sure no one was hiding inside. None of the scarecrows flinched.

Then I glanced at the far field. I saw a lone scarecrow that was very different from all the others. This scarecrow was covered in big black crows!

The birds were perched along its raggedy arms. Their heads were tilted as though they were listening to something. Then the scarecrow suddenly nodded its head, and the crows all took to the sky!

Uh Oh!

The birds hadn't flown very high when they turned in midair and dive-bombed straight into the long grass of the meadow! The crows had vanished, but I could still see their tracks as they beat a path through the grass.

They were heading for our picnic basket!

I dashed across the meadow, hoping to head off the tracks of ruffled grass as the crows charged toward our tree. It was neck and neck as we both drew closer. Then I leaped forward and landed at the edge of the blanket. I'd blocked the crows' path. They had no choice but to take to the sky again. They shot out of the grass like feathered rockets.

CAW!
CAW!
CAW!

They left, flapping away angrily.

I turned to make sure Mom was OK. I was relieved to find her fast asleep with the book over her face. Then I marched down the hill toward the weird scarecrow with the angry crows now circling above it.

The scarecrow didn't move when I approached. In fact, it looked as innocent as all the others. But I'd already seen it nodding. I knew there was *someone* lurking inside, so I pulled out my pencil.

I don't jab people with pointy things if I can help it. I thought I'd give the crook a chance to surrender first.

"Give yourself up!" I said, waving the pencil at him.

Nothing.

"It's very pointy!" I added, tapping the point with the tip of my finger.

Nothing.

"Well, don't say I didn't warn you!" I said and jabbed the scarecrow in the leg.

I immediately jumped back, expecting the scarecrow to yelp or yell or jump down and chase me across the field. But like all the other scarecrows, it didn't even flinch.

I stepped forward again and gave his brown pants a few more jabs just to be sure.

Nothing.

When I got no response, I grabbed the legs and gave them a prod and a squeeze to discover they were just a pair of old jeans stuffed full of straw. Then I poked its belly and found that it was full of straw too. Finally, I reached up to find that it had saggy straw arms and twigs for fingers.

It was obvious this was just a regular scarecrow. I decided that the wind must have blown its sack head forward. That scared the crows away and made it *look* like a nod. . . .

"Have you quite finished prodding me?" said the scarecrow. It tilted its head to peer down at me through two button eyes! "Because poking a scarecrow is very rude, you know."

"ARRRGH!"

I yelled and darted back a few steps.

"And now you're screaming at me," sighed the scarecrow. It shook its head from side to side with disapproval. Then it glanced up into the sky at the circling crows and whistled a command. Suddenly the crows all started dive-bombing again. This time they were heading straight for me!

So I sprinted across the field toward
the other scarecrows. I hoped the
birds might actually be scared of these
ones. But as I got nearer, they didn't
seem bothered at all.

I ripped down the nearest
scarecrow and pulled on its ratty hat
and straw-filled sweater. And I did
it just in time because one of the
crows pecked my arm with its beak.

The other
birds
swooped down
and pecked
at me too,
but the hat
and stuffed
sweater protected
me from their jabbing beaks. Then I
flapped my arms around like a lunatic
until the startled birds flew off.

"PHEW!" I sighed, scratching
my itchy head through the hat.

The scarecrow obviously
thought it was clever, using the birds
to pay me back for prodding him
with the pencil, but there was still
one thing about all this that just didn't
make sense.

SCARECROWS CAN'T TALK!

I've seen some weird things during my time as a secret agent, but there has always been a rational explanation behind everything. I know for a fact that scarecrows can't talk, which meant I needed to have a serious conversation with this one!

I decided to grab my backpack first because I still didn't know who or what I was dealing with. I might need a gadget to get me out of a sticky situation—*or* something heavy to swing at the nasty birds!

Unfortunately, Mom was lying on one of the straps of my backpack.

When I tugged it free, her book slipped down her face and her eyes popped open. She was still half-asleep and gazed up at me though sleepy eyes.

"Afternoon, Ma'am," I said quickly, tipping my hat politely. "I'm just off to scare some crows," I added cheerily, prodding my fat straw belly.

Then I hurried away doing a silly scarecrow walk.

My mom always takes ages to wake up in the morning, so I hoped my bizarre behavior would make her think she was dreaming. I whipped out my mirror-on-a-stick gadget and held it up to look behind me. I saw Mom frown for a moment and then fall back to sleep.

PHEW!

By the time I got back to the talking scarecrow I was pretty annoyed.

"Now listen here!" I snapped, waving a finger at him.

"I know that scarecrows can't talk or nod their heads or send their nasty little birds after a young girl who is just trying to protect her picnic. . . ."

"Really?" interrupted the scarecrow.

"Yes, *really*!" I said, dumping my backpack in the grass.

"Then why are you having a conversation with one?" The scarecrow chuckled.

"Because there's something else going on here. I'm going to get to the bottom of it!" I said, rolling up my sleeves and taking a step forward.

"You picked the wrong picnic this time, Mister!"

"What are you doing?" gasped the scarecrow. "Get away from me!"

I ignored the scarecrow's protests. I began tugging at his legs, practically swinging on them to loosen the waist knot. Eventually I managed to pull them free, and they landed with a soft thud on the grass. Then I picked up the jeans and shook them upside down.

"Hey!"

said the
scarecrow.

"Those are
my legs!"

"Hmmm?"
I said, picking
through the straw
to find a few sandwiches.

Next, I grabbed the hem of
his shirt. I pulled hard with my foot
propped against the vertical post for
leverage. The horizontal post ran
through the sleeves, and it took all
my strength to rip it.

"Stop that!" yelled the scarecrow. "I'm already legless, leave me my body!"

"It's not your *body*," I grunted, straining with the effort. "It's just rags and straw and stolen food!" I added. Eventually the torso tumbled down and landed at my feet. When I popped open the shirt buttons, I found a squished cake and an apple pie among the straw.

"Now what have you got to say for yourself?" I said, pointing at the food.

The head leaned forward and peered down at the evidence.

"I have to admit, it doesn't look good," it said.

"Oh, I haven't finished yet," I said, rummaging in my backpack.

I pulled out my extendable grabber-hand gadget and waved it at what was left of the scarecrow.  The head had been pretty chatty all the time it thought it was out of my reach. Now it simply quivered on its post.

"Anything to say before I pull your head off?" I said, extending the hand and knocking its hat off. Then I closed the hand over the head sack of the scarecrow. "Any last words?"

"Who's a pretty boy then?" said the scarecrow, as I pulled its head off.

I have to admit, I was a bit worried about what I might find under the sack. When I peered up

to find a brightly
colored parrot
perched on the post,
I was more confused than
anything else.

"You're a parrot!" I
gasped.

"Polly's the name,"
it said, bobbing its *real* head. "Pleased to
meet you."

I was about to quiz the parrot when I became aware of the crows cawing overhead. They seemed very angry and began dropping in a familiar dive-bomb formation. But this time Polly hadn't whistled a signal.

"UH OH!" said the parrot, looking up nervously.

"Call them off!" I yelled, grabbing my backpack ready to fend off the beaks.

"They won't listen to me now that they've seen I'm just a bird," squawked Polly. "That's why I hid inside the scarecrow. And now that they know I tricked them, I think they want all the food for themselves."

CAW! CAW! CAW!

As the crows swooped down, the frightened parrot fluttered onto my shoulder. I realized how small he was. I couldn't leave Polly to the nasty crows, so I began whirling my backpack over my head as I ran across the field.

A few of the birds followed us, giving warning caws, but they soon rejoined the rest of the flock squabbling over the fallen food.

Away from the pecking beaks, the parrot thanked me for rescuing him.

I dressed the scarecrow whose clothes I'd borrowed. Then, the parrot told me how he ended up inside a scarecrow's head, training crows to steal food for him.

Polly's owner was a college professor who had taught him loads of clever words to say. The professor quickly discovered that his parrot was much *smarter* than the average bird. Polly said he liked living with the professor because he wasn't kept in a cage and could fly around freely. But one day he'd flown too far and couldn't find his way home again.

"I thought birds were really good at finding their way home?" I said.

"I'm not a homing pigeon," said Polly. "But I do know my address."

"Then couldn't you just ask someone for directions?" I suggested.

"The professor told me not to talk to strangers," said the parrot. "He said that people wouldn't expect a bird to be smart enough to hold a conversation and that I might end up in the wrong hands."

"Yeah," I said. "He's probably right about that."

"I could ask *you* for directions!" said the parrot, excitedly.

"I'm not sure how I would explain it to my mom though. . . ." I said, looking over at the tree. It was then that I noticed Mom had woken up and was waving at me to come and have lunch. "Hang on a minute," I said, pulling out the paper and my pointy pencil.

"ARRRGH!"  squawked the parrot.

"I'm not going to stab you," I laughed. "Give me your address. . . ."

Luckily, Mom bought the story
about finding the parrot with a note
tied to his leg. She said we'd look
up the address on the map and drive
him home after lunch. Then, as she
unpacked the picnic, Mom told me
all about the strange scarecrow dream
she'd had.

"A talking scarecrow!" she
chuckled. "Can you imagine?"

"Hmmm . . ." I said, peering over my sunglasses at a guilty-looking Polly.

Mom laid out the sandwiches and cake. She frowned at the parrot perched on the edge of the picnic basket. "Do you think it would be OK to feed him?" she asked, pulling off a piece of cake.

Polly was gazing at the lump of cake. I could tell he really wanted to say "YES, PLEASE!" But I'd warned him not to speak in front of Mom, just in case she got freaked out.

"I think he'd like that," I smiled.

The Case of the Gobbledygook Books

I often go to the school library during lunchtime and have my sandwich with Ms. Young, the librarian. Ms. Young is really nice and sets aside books for me that have anything to do with secret agents. At the moment, I'm into a series called Suzy Spy. Suzy is a secret agent who travels the world fighting crime. She gets to use brilliant gadgets that the government makes for her.

This particular lunchtime, I went to the library hoping to get the latest Suzy Spy book, *Peril in Paris!* The librarian had said it would come on Monday morning and that she would happily put it aside for me.

When I entered the library, Ms. Young was nowhere to be seen. Standing behind her counter was a large woman with square glasses and short bangs.

I'm always suspicious when a new staff member joins the school because you never know when or where someone might try to take over the world. So I approached with caution and tipped my sunglasses.

"Where's the librarian?" I asked.

"If you're referring to the timid little bookworm who *used* to work here, she's retired!" said the woman, typing frantically on her laptop. "You'll be dealing with me from now on. My name is Ms. Rogue."

My secret-agent senses immediately kicked in.

First of all, Ms. Young was much too *young* to retire. And even if she had, she would definitely have said good-bye to me before leaving. Then there was the new librarian's ridiculous name! Evil geniuses and criminal masterminds often change their names to make them sound more villainous. Ms. *Rogue* was the worst made-up name I'd ever heard.

It was then that I noticed the
sound of Ms. Rogue's typing was
echoed through the library. When
I looked around, I saw the reading
tables were all bunched together and
had brand-new laptops on them.

The laptops were identical to the one
she was using. The kids sitting at the
keyboards were all typing at the same
lightning speed.

I casually slid along the counter and leaned forward to get a look at Ms. Rogue's screen. But before I could see what she was typing, she slammed the thing shut and glared at me.

"Is there something I can help you with?" she snapped. She drummed her fingers impatiently on the top of the laptop. "As you can see, I'm very busy, er . . . networking all the new library computers."

Being a
secret agent, I'm
used to dealing
with strange
characters. I was
sure Ms. Rogue
was doing more
than just linking a few
laptops. But I couldn't
let her know I was on to her. I uttered
the first thing that came into my
head.

"Suzy Spy!"
I said.

"Excuse
me?"
said the
librarian.

"The new Suzy Spy book," I explained. "Ms. Young said she'd put it aside for me."

"Oh, I'm afraid that one has already been checked out," said Ms. Rogue. "A delightful young girl took it this morning. She said she already has the whole collection at home but didn't want to crease their spines. . . ."

Suddenly, the library doors
swung open and Trudy Hart entered.
Her face was buried in *Peril in Paris!* I
should have known my arch nemesis
had nabbed the book, but the word
"delightful" had thrown me. Trudy
knows how much I love the Suzy Spy
books. I was fully expecting her to
gloat about getting the new one first.

As Trudy walked past, she paused for a moment and frowned as though she didn't know who I was. Then she smiled pleasantly and sat at one of the new computers. The Trudy Hart I know *never* passes up an opportunity to gloat. Something *seriously* strange was going on. . . .

"Would you like to read this one instead?" the librarian said suddenly, holding up a book called *Poochie Power!*

She was wearing a smile that looked very uncomfortable on her face. "It's about a doggie with magical powers. It's *very* funny."

"No thanks, I think I'll look for something else," I said, strolling away and heading for the bookshelves behind Trudy Hart. I pretended to browse the books until the librarian reopened her laptop and resumed her frantic typing. Then I peered over Trudy's shoulder.

Trudy had placed the book beside her and was tapping away on the keyboard along with all the other kids. Her fingers were a blur of manic movement! But when I looked at the screen, I saw that she was typing gobbledygook!

Then I glanced at the Suzy Spy book. Instead of the usual

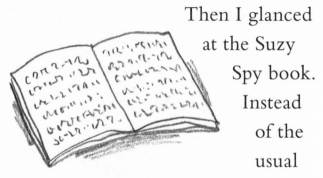

opening chapter that always begins with the words "Hi! My name is Suzy Spy. . . ," the page was also filled with gobbledygook!

Even glancing at the page made me feel a bit odd, which meant

the gobbledygook obviously wasn't gobbledygook at all. What looked like nonsense to me was probably responsible for turning Trudy into a human robot. (That was *actually* a bit of an improvement!)

A quick squint at the other kids' books confirmed that their pages had also been swapped for the mysterious language. The kids were typing the exact same thing on their laptops, fingers jabbing at the keys like little pistons.

Then I suddenly realized where
I had seen this kind of writing before!

It was a few weeks before in
tech class. My computer had crashed,
and loads of random letters and
numbers and symbols had appeared on
the screen. I'd asked the tech teacher
what this was, and he explained that
it was a special language that told
computers what to do.

The kids around the tables had all been reading the same gobbledygook in their books, and now they were acting like rapid-typing robots. All this *had* to mean they were being told what to do in computer language.

I peered over my sunglasses and saw that Ms. Rogue was looking over her laptop at me. She was getting suspicious. I had to find a way to blend in with the weird robot kids.

 I pulled a couple of books from the shelf and checked the pages. They all had regular words in them. The librarian was handing out the gobbledygook books herself. Like the one she had offered me. . . .

I strolled back to the counter and smiled sweetly.

"Um, I can't find anything interesting, so I'd like to read the book about the magic doggie, please," I said. I hoped Ms. Rogue was keen to add another soldier to her creepy robot army.

The librarian grinned from ear to ear as she passed me the book.

A quick glance inside confirmed that *Poochie Power!* was another of Ms. Rogue's gobbledygook books. I took it to a chair tucked away behind a bookshelf. I wasn't sure how long the brain programming was supposed to take, so I waited five minutes. Then I wandered out again like a robot.

I sat down at one of the empty laptops, stared straight ahead, and began tapping randomly at the keys as fast as I could. Then, keeping my head still, I glanced sideways. A very smug-looking librarian was peeping over the counter.

I'd obviously fooled her. Now I had to figure out exactly what she was up to.

I slipped a hand down to the mouse and clicked around the desktop until I found a folder called "TOP SECRET." And when I opened the folder, I found a document called "My Fiendish Plan."

"That's original!" I mumbled, clicking the file open.

 I've foiled lots of plans to take over the world before, but this lunatic librarian was planning to take over the World Wide Web! This didn't tell me what she planned to do if she succeeded, but businesses use the Internet and lots of people have it at home. She'd probably be able to access anything she wanted!

Ms. Rogue suddenly left her counter. She marched toward the reading tables where I was still snooping and everyone else was typing. I quickly got rid of the folder and resumed the random prodding of keys.

"Someone here is typing gobbledygook!" she yelled, banging her fist on the table. The sudden bang made me jump, which was a huge mistake. None of the other kids even reacted to the noise, and Ms. Rogue now knew I was faking.

The librarian lurched forward and made a grab for me, but I managed to duck under the table. I escaped through Trudy Hart's legs.

I jumped up at the other side of the table to find Ms. Rogue tapping at my laptop, deleting what I'd typed. This proved that the robot kids were *not* just jabbing keys at random. They were turbo-typing the code that would allow Ms. Rogue to take over the Internet!

"You're not going to get away with this!" I said, waving a finger across the table.

"And who's going to stop me?" said the librarian, snapping the laptop shut.

"Me!" I said confidently, although I still had no idea how.

As Ms. Rogue chased me around the tables, I pressed DELETE on all of the other kids' computers, hoping it might undo their programming or something like that.

But it had no effect at all. They just continued to type.

The librarian was gaining on me, so I broke away and charged across the library. I ducked down aisles of books that were a bit narrow for someone as big as my pursuer—which at least slowed her down a bit.

But wherever I went, Ms. Rogue was
still behind me. I spotted the storage
closet up ahead and sprinted for it.

Luckily, the door wasn't locked.
I managed to barge inside and slam
the door shut before she caught me. I
bolted the door and peeped through
the blind. Ms. Rogue was stomping
her massive feet and cursing my escape.

Then I became aware of another voice coming from *inside* the room!

"Mmmf mmf fmm!" it went, which was pretty creepy.

I turned around very slowly to find Ms. Young sitting in the middle of the room! The *real* librarian was tied to a chair and had a date-stamp sticker stuck over her mouth. I hurried forward and ripped it off quickly like a Band-Aid.

"Amelia!" gasped Ms. Young. "Oh, thank goodness!"

"Are you OK, Ms. Young?" I asked. I quickly began untying the ropes. "I guess you already know a madwoman has taken over the library! What happened?"

"I came in early this morning to unpack the new delivery of books," she explained. "And as soon as I stepped through the door, a large woman with unfortunate bangs pounced on me and tied me up. Then she stuffed me in here!"

"Did she say anything?" I asked, undoing the last of the knots.

"Well, she did seem very irritated that there were so many books. Which I thought was odd. This is a library, after all," said Ms. Young, rubbing her wrists. "In fact, she spent the whole time ranting about how useless books were. . . ."

"Evil geniuses and criminal masterminds do love to rant," I said, stepping back over to the door.

Through the blind I could see Ms. Rogue had returned to the laptop at the counter and was typing even more furiously than before.

"Evil geniuses and criminal masterminds?" frowned Ms. Young.

"Er, yes . . ." I said, suddenly realizing I'd said too much.

I couldn't let the librarian know I was a secret agent because then it wouldn't be secret anymore. "I mean they always love to rant in the Suzy Spy books."

"Of course," said Ms. Young, joining me at the door and looking through the blind. "Perhaps she really *is* an evil genius or a criminal mastermind! I wonder what she's doing on that laptop?"

"I'm not sure, but I think she's trying to take over the Internet," I said, trying to sound vague and clueless. "She also tampered with the books to make the kids write her computer code. . . ."

"Tampered with my books!" gasped Ms. Young.

I was wondering how I could stop the fake librarian *and* keep the real librarian safe—all without revealing my secret-agent identity, when Ms. Young suddenly unlocked the door and charged into the library!

Uh Oh!

I ran after the librarian, who was heading straight for Ms. Rogue!

"Stop what you're doing and leave my library right now!" demanded Ms. Young.

The fake librarian narrowed her eyes at the real librarian and then laughed. It was a loud booming laugh that I've heard many times before. It's the lunatic laugh of someone who thinks a plan for world domination is unstoppable.

I stood next to Ms. Young and decided to speed things along a bit.

"So what *are* you trying to do anyway?" I sighed. Evil geniuses and criminal masterminds simply can't resist bragging about how clever they are. "Aside from taking over the Internet, of course!"

"I plan to rid the world of books!" said Ms. Rogue, flinging her arms in the air dramatically. "And when I've closed down every library and bookstore and publisher, I will then be able to control what everyone reads on the Internet!"

Ms. Young gasped. I scratched my head.

"What have you got against books?" I asked. I was stalling while I figured out what to do next.

"They are dusty and outdated, and the people who read them are weak and dull!" growled Ms. Rogue. "We live in an age of the information superhighway! With megabits and gigabits and downloads and upgrades. . . ."

Ms. Rogue lost track of her rant for a moment because she had suddenly lost half her audience. Ms. Young had hurried away and seemed

 to be hiding behind one of the bookshelves.

"And that's the perfect example!" sneered Ms. Rogue, pointing to the empty spot where Ms. Young had been standing. "Surrounding herself with all these dusty books has turned her into a timid little mouse who flees at the first sign of. . . ."

Ms. Young suddenly reappeared with a large book. Ms. Rogue looked completely baffled as the librarian approached the counter. I was pretty confused about Ms. Young's book too.

"This is the complete works of William Shakespeare!" Ms. Young stated proudly. "Probably the greatest writer in the history of the world!" She lifted the open book in preparation for a reading.

Ms. Rogue was about to stifle an exaggerated yawn when Ms. Young suddenly raised the book higher. Then she snapped it shut and brought the massive volume down on the laptop with an almighty

BANG!

Ms. Rogue's yawn quickly became a scream as the keys and wires and other broken bits flew out of her laptop and scattered everywhere. Then a puff of black smoke rose from the crushed computer.

Ms. Rogue's defeated scream was followed by a moment of silence. We heard no key tapping from the kids on the reading tables. They were all frowning, except for Trudy who was glaring. Smashing the computer had definitely broken the spell. Then they turned to the source of the scream with fingers pressed to their lips.

"*SHHHHHHHH!*" they all hissed together.

SHHHHHHHH!

Ms. Rogue looked startled for a moment. Then she fixed her sights on Ms. Young. Suddenly the large lunatic vaulted over the counter and chased the librarian into the storage closet. The door slammed shut behind them.

UH OH! I thought, as the sounds of banging and crashing echoed through the library. Moments later, the door opened. Ms. Rogue was tied to the chair with a "PROPERTY OF THE LIBRARY" sticker on her mouth!

"But how..." I gasped. Ms. Young left the room dusting off her hands.

"I read the Suzy Spy books too," smiled the librarian. "Do you remember what happened in *Menace in Milan*?"

"It's one of my favorites," I said. I remembered how Suzy circled the crook with a rope like a cowboy and tied him to an office chair.

This was obviously how the nimble librarian had overpowered Ms. Rogue.

"Speaking of which . . ." said Ms. Young.

The librarian went behind the counter and pulled out a brand-new copy of *Peril in Paris!* She handed it to me with a smile. Then she quickly gathered up the gobbledygook books from the tables.

Trudy was about to protest
when Ms. Young took *her* book, but
then she decided against it. I think
Trudy stopped liking the Suzy Spy
books that day.

When the police came to take Ms. Rogue away, they applauded Ms. Young for her extraordinary skill and bravery in defeating the criminal. The librarian laughed and said she felt like a real secret agent!

Then I sat down with my lunch and started reading the latest Suzy Spy book.

I was really looking forward to finding out what trouble she'd found in Paris. Sometimes it's really nice to let someone else save the world for a change.

AGENT Amelia

Check out my other books!

Three more fabulously funny stories in each book.

Agent Amelia
#1

Ghost Diamond!

A jewel with a world-dominating spirit, a plague of furry cat burglars, and a criminal mastermind with a creepy weed army—Agent Amelia just has to get busy to save the world!

Agent Amelia
#2
Zombie COWS!

Mechanical farm animals, a modern-day Pied Piper, and a case of exploding cakes—Agent Amelia has a lot on her plate as she fights to save the world!

Agent Amelia
#3
Hypno Hounds!

A deserted village haunted by handbag hounds, a mad science teacher hiding experimental pom-pom creatures, and some thieving roller-skating teddies. It's enough to keep Amelia busy, saving the world!

Agent Amelia
#4

Spooky Ballet!

A batty ballet teacher, a librarian who hates books, and parrot picnic pirate! With villains like these, it's a good thing Agent Amelia is on duty.